Nature Watch

Outdoor Activities

CONTENTS

	TIME NEEDED	PAGE

BUSH DETECTIVES

NATURE WATCH

SMALL WONDERS

Tree-frog

Nature activities

Are you looking for some fantastic ideas that will get you out of the house and into the great outdoors? If so, this book is perfect for you. It is jam-packed with interesting nature-based things to make and do. It will enable you to learn new skills and make your own discoveries about the natural world that surrounds you. Not only that, but there are great tips for having loads of holiday fun.

Become a "bush detective" or a "nature watcher" and investigate the tremendous variety of living things that share your world. Use nature as your inspiration as you create useful tools to observe animals safely without disturbing them. All this and more awaits you inside this amazing book.

Brushtail possum

Mantid

On your doorstep

You don't have to go far to become a nature watcher. Nature comes to you. Even in your backyard there are plenty of animals to see. From tiny insects to the birds that visit every day, you can watch animals on your own doorstep.

Cockatoo

2

... and in the bush

If you travel a little further, you might see some well-known Aussie animals, like kangaroos and koalas. If you are lucky, you might even be able to take a picture of one and show all your friends.

Kangaroo

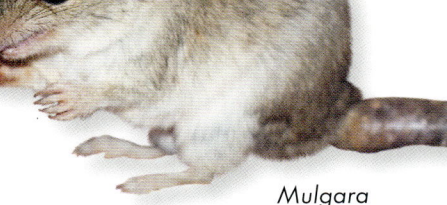

Get ready to go wild!

Mulgara

One way to see animals in their natural habitat is to go bushwalking. There are more hiding places for wildlife in the bush than in the city. If you go bushwalking, here are some important things to take with you. Making a checklist will help you remember them all.

SHOES & SOCKS
Wear a pair of comfortable sneakers with good grip on the soles. Make sure they don't give you blisters and wear thick socks to protect your feet.

BACKPACK WITH WATER & FOOD
Take a backpack to carry your food, water and other gear. Binoculars can also be useful for nature watching.

SUNSMART GEAR
Don't forget to SLIP (on a shirt), SLOP (on sunscreen), SLAP (on a hat), SEEK (the shade) and SLIDE (on your sunglasses).

FIRST AID KIT
Always carry a first aid kit when you go bushwalking just in case there is an accident.

Echidna

Where are you going?

It's best to go bushwalking with an adult who knows the area. Before heading off, even with an adult, tell someone at home where you are going and what time you will be coming back.

Shhh! The animals may hear you coming!

Take a notebook & pencil

A notebook and pencil are very useful for recording the animals you see. Write down the animal's name, where you saw it, what time of day you saw it, what it was doing and any other interesting facts.

Let's make tracks

Lace monitor

Wombat

While you are walking along bush trails, look out for animal tracks. Unfortunately, if the ground is hard or rocky animals won't leave behind many footprints. If the ground is muddy, soft or sandy, you may be rewarded by seeing lots of animal tracks. The best way to keep a record of the tracks you see is to take a plaster cast of them. You can even make a cast of your own footprints.

Things you will need ...

Taking a plaster cast of animal tracks is easy, but if you can't find some real animal tracks try casting your own hand- or footprints. You will need the following materials to make the cast:

- A strip of cardboard 50 centimetres long by 5 centimetres wide (to stop the plaster leaking out)
- A paperclip • A mixing bowl
- Paper towel • Water
- A packet of plaster of Paris
- A spoon or popsicle stick (for stirring)

Bilby

How good are you at tracking?

An animal's tracks can give you a lot of information. The shape of each footprint can tell you what kind of animal made the tracks. The depth can tell you how heavy the animal may be. The distance between the prints can tell you how fast it was travelling.

Turtle tracks

What to do ...

1 Bend the cardboard strip around the footprint or animal track so that it makes a ring wall. Use the paperclip to hold the ends of the cardboard together. Push the cardboard wall down into the soft ground, trying not to break up the footprint.

2 In the mixing bowl, add one-third of a cup of water to two-thirds of a cup of plaster. Stir thoroughly so you don't get any lumps. The mixture should be thick but runny, like honey. Add more water if it is too thick.

3 When you've finished stirring, gently pour the plaster and water mixture into the cardboard ring. Don't pour the mixture directly onto the footprint or you might damage it, instead pour the plaster mixture to the side of the track and let it ooze into the footprint. Fill the inside of the cardboard ring to a depth of about 2 centimetres. Lay a paper towel across the top of the mixture to make the surface of the plaster strong.

4 Let the plaster set for about one hour, then check that it is quite hard before trying to lift it. Take care picking up the cast in case it breaks. Wait for at least another day for the plaster to harden further before washing off any dirt.

Guess what?

Tiger snake

Can you guess what kind of animal made these tracks? Answers are on page 32.

1.

2.

3.

4.

5.

Animal scratches

Brushtail possum

Animals that climb, like koalas and possums, have sharp claws. As they climb, they dig their claws into the bark to get a good grip. This often leaves scratches, especially on smooth-barked trees like gum trees. Look for such scratches whenever you go bushwalking. They will give you clues as to what animals may be hiding in the branches. To record the scratches, you can photograph them or take a "rubbing" from them. Rubbings give an exact copy of the scratches so you can later show an expert who may be able to identify the animals.

Things you will need ...

Rubbings work best on smooth-barked trees. It is almost impossible to get a good rubbing from a rough-barked tree. You will need the following materials:

- A smooth-barked tree with animal scratches
- A sheet of plain white paper (A4 or A3)
- A colouring pencil (any dark colour — brown, black or blue is best)

Fresh scratches or old?

Favoured trees will often have several scratches from many animals or from the same animal that has returned to the tree many times. You can tell how fresh each scratch is by looking at its colour. Pale, red or brown scratches are more recent than dark grey marks.

1. The first task is to find a tree with plenty of animal claw marks in the bark. This will be easier than you think. Possums often visit trees growing in the suburbs of towns and cities. You have probably seen these marks on the bark of some local trees and didn't realise they may have been made by a possum or koala.

2. Place the sheet of paper over the scratches on the bark and press it down firmly, to stop it from moving.

3. Use the colouring pencil and begin colouring in a section of the paper. Make long strokes with the side of the pencil tip, as if you were shading. Don't press too hard or the paper will tear.

When complete, your rubbing might look a little like the picture on the left. It will be a record of the exact shape and size of the original scratches on the tree.

Rubbing

Koalas

Let me give you a hand

Look at the scratches on the tree above. Notice that you can often see two long scratches close together and running parallel. These two scratches were made by the two thumb claws on the hand of a koala.

Bandicoots

Make your own compass

It is easy to get lost in the bush. That's why many bushwalkers carry maps and a compass. A compass helps people navigate by showing them the directions of north, south, east and west. The needle of the compass is magnetised and always points to the North Pole. You can make your own compass by magnetising a pin.

Things you will need ...

You should be able to find most of the materials you need at home, except for the magnet. A bar magnet works best. You can get one from a novelty store or toy shop.

- A pin or a needle (careful — it may be sharp)
- A magnet
- A bowl of water
- A small square of paper

A very big magnet!

Did you know that the Earth is really a giant magnet? It has a north and a south pole. A compass is also a magnet. One end of the compass needle is attracted to the North Pole of the Earth and the other end to the South Pole of the Earth.

1 Place a bowl of water on the table and let the water settle. Hold the head of the pin between your thumb and finger. Stroke the magnet against the pin, starting near the pin's head and stroking towards the sharp end. You may have to do this fifty or sixty times, always stroking in the same direction.

2 Now float a small square of paper in the bowl of water and gently place the pin on top of the floating paper. Allow a few seconds until the pin and paper stop spinning. The paper will then sink, leaving the pin behind.

3 When it is still, the pin should be pointing in a north–south direction. To figure out if the sharp end is pointing north or south, you will have to wait until the afternoon. Stand so that you are facing the direction in which the sharp end is pointing. If it is pointing north, the afternoon sun will be on your left side. If it is pointing south, the afternoon sun will be on your right side.

Compass

A Compass Can be Fooled

Placing a magnet near a compass can make the needle point in the wrong direction. Instead of pointing to the Earth's north pole, it will point to the magnet's north pole. A magnet near a ship's compass could be disastrous!

The Maheno shipwreck, sunk in 1935 on the coastline of Fraser Island

11

Green tree python

Directions from the sun

If you don't have a compass and don't have the materials to make one, you can still figure out where north, south, east and west are located. All you need is a shadow cast by a fence post, stick or tall tree. Here is how to do it.

1 Carefully push the end of a stick into the ground so it stands up straight without falling. (If the ground is too hard, you can use the shadow cast by any vertical object, like a fence post or a tree.)

2 If the sun is shining, the stick or fence post will cast a shadow. Mark where the tip of the shadow falls on the ground.

3 As the sun travels from east to west across the sky, it makes the shadow move. After a couple of hours, make another mark where the tip of the shadow now falls.

4 Connect the two positions you have just marked by drawing a straight line on the ground between them. Alternatively, lay a straight stick across the marks.

Where is the sun?

You can tell what the time is by checking where the sun is in the sky. If the sun is at its highest point in the middle of the sky, it is midday or 12.00 noon. This is one of the most important times of the day — lunch time!

5 Stand with your toes on the line so that the first mark is on your left and the second mark is on your right.

6 Directly ahead of you is north. Behind you is south. To your left is west and to your right is east.

This is a way of measuring the approximate location of the compass points. Your approximation will be more accurate if you use a very tall stick rather than a short one. It will also be more accurate if you wait for a longer period of time between marking the tips of the shadow. It can be done at any time of the day no matter where you are. The sun just needs to shine and make shadows on the ground.

N

W E

S

finding direction at sunset

Did you know that the sun sets in the west? At sunset, stretch your arms out as in this photograph. If you point your left hand at the setting sun, your right hand will be pointing east and you will be looking to the north.

Crimson chat

30 MINS

Superb fairy-wren

Setting up a bird hide

Like most animals, birds can be very shy. They will fly away if they see you spying on them. If you want to see birds without them seeing you, you can build a bird hide. It is called a "hide", because once you are inside it, you are hidden from view and the birds will act as if you weren't there.

Scarlet robin

Hides are like cubby houses and it can be a lot of fun building one. Start by finding out where the birds that you want to watch are gathered. You will build your hide as close to this place as possible without disturbing the birds.

It is usually best to build your hide using lightweight materials so you can move it if you have to. All the hide has to do is hide you for long enough for you to birdwatch.

Palm cockatoo

Kookaburras

What's "kooking"?

Some birds get used to having people around, so you don't need a hide to watch them. Kookaburras stay close to camping grounds and picnic tables, hoping to steal a sausage or two. Unfortunately, human food isn't always very healthy for birds to eat so it is best not to feed them.

Here are some ideas for making a hide

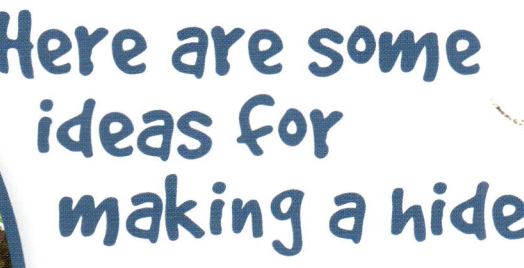

Rainbow bee-eater

SHEET HIDE

All you need for this hide is an old sheet or blanket and some rope. Stretch out a rope along the ground. Lay the sheet on top of the rope and place some rocks on the corners of the sheet. Lift the rope and tie each end to a tree or branch. Then sprinkle leaves on the sheet so it looks like part of the ground. Crawl inside and wait for the birds to arrive.

CARDBOARD BOX HIDE

Sometimes you can find old cardboard packing boxes at your local shops. The best boxes are those that are used to pack refrigerators, since they will be big enough for you to crawl inside. All you have to do is sprinkle dirt and leaves on the outside. You might like to cut out some small windows in the sides to peek through.

If you don't want to build your own hide, you can visit a national park or public wetland reserve that has a bird hide already built. Birds don't pay any attention to hides because, to them, hides are just part of the scenery.

Happy hideout

Permanent buildings attract insects, spiders, geckoes and mice and these animals attract birds. Sometimes the very best hide can be your own home. All you have to do is look out of the window.

15

Bird Feeder

Why not build a bird feeding station to encourage birds to your backyard? They are so simple to make and you can learn so much about birds by watching their behaviour at the feeder.

Bee-eater

Honeyeater

Things you will need...

This feeder provides small birds with a place to perch while they eat the food inside.

- An empty, plastic soft drink bottle (with lid)
- Two sticks or pieces of dowel 25–30 centimetres long
- 1 metre length of string or cord
- Mixed grain birdseed
- A small screwdriver or sharp spike
- A pair of scissors

Red wattlebird

What do birds like?

What do the birds in your garden eat? To find out, make two or more feeders. Place seed in one and fruit in another. You could even place some flowers in the feeder to see if they attract any visitors.

Lorikeet

What to do ...

1 Rinse the soft drink bottle with clean water and allow it to dry. Then, with a screwdriver or sharp spike, punch four holes through opposite sides of the bottom section of the plastic bottle. Make sure that one set of holes is lower than the other.

2 Push the sticks or dowel through the holes so they poke out on both sides of the bottle. These will be the perches for birds that visit the feeder.

3 With a pair of sharp scissors, cut windows in the bottle as shown. The windows need to be large enough for the birds to pop their heads through to eat the seed in the bottle.

4 Add seed to the bottle, up to the level of the windows. Then tie both ends of the string to the neck of the bottle. Hang it from the branch of a tree where you can watch the visiting birds without disturbing them.

Magpie

Keep it clean & dry

You should check the feeder every day to make sure the seed isn't wet or mouldy and to add fresh food. It is also a good idea to wash the feeder regularly. Diseases can be spread from one bird to another at feeders. Keeping the feeders dry and clean helps minimise this risk.

Twenty birds to find

Most people can recognise an emu or a kookaburra but they might not know the names of the many small birds that visit their gardens every day. On these pages you will find the photographs and names of some birds that may visit your area. If you see one of these birds in your neighbourhood, place a tick in the circle next to its photograph.

Kookaburra

Willie wagtail

Peewee

Butcherbird

Magpie

Swallow

Silver gull

Raven

Galah

Cockatiel

Rainbow lorikeet

Goshawk

Turtle-dove

Crested pigeon

Ibis

Heron

Egret

Friarbird

Noisy miner

Masked lapwing

Score 5 points for every bird spotted
— see if you can score 100 points.

My score:

/100

Black-shouldered kite

Make a "hawk" kite

Eagles and hawks seem to soar through the sky without flapping their wings. You can make a kite that can do the same. Once built, you can fly it in your backyard. You could even take it to the park or beach, but hang on tight or the wind might carry it away.

Things you will need ...

- A 52 centimetre square sheet of **clear** plastic polythene (ask at the hardware store). Alternatively, use a very large clear plastic bag or bin liner

- A sheet of coloured contact

- A hole punch
- Insulation tape

- Scissors or craft knife
- Tape measure

- A texta or permanent marker

- A ball of string (at least 20 metres)

- Two 50 centimetre lengths of thin wooden dowel or bamboo

- Hawk template printed at the back of this book

You may need an adult to help do the cutting tasks in this activity.

Brown goshawk

Wedge-tailed eagle

Shapes in the sky

Small birds quickly learn to recognise the silhouette of a hawk soaring overhead. If they get caught in the open, they can soon become the hawk's next meal.

Mark the centre point

15 cm

Cut Cut

Cut

Cut

Mark the centre point

Punch holes in the tape here

Punch holes in the tape here

Flip the kite over

Tie string to dowel on the other side of the kite

Tie a loop above where the pieces of dowel cross

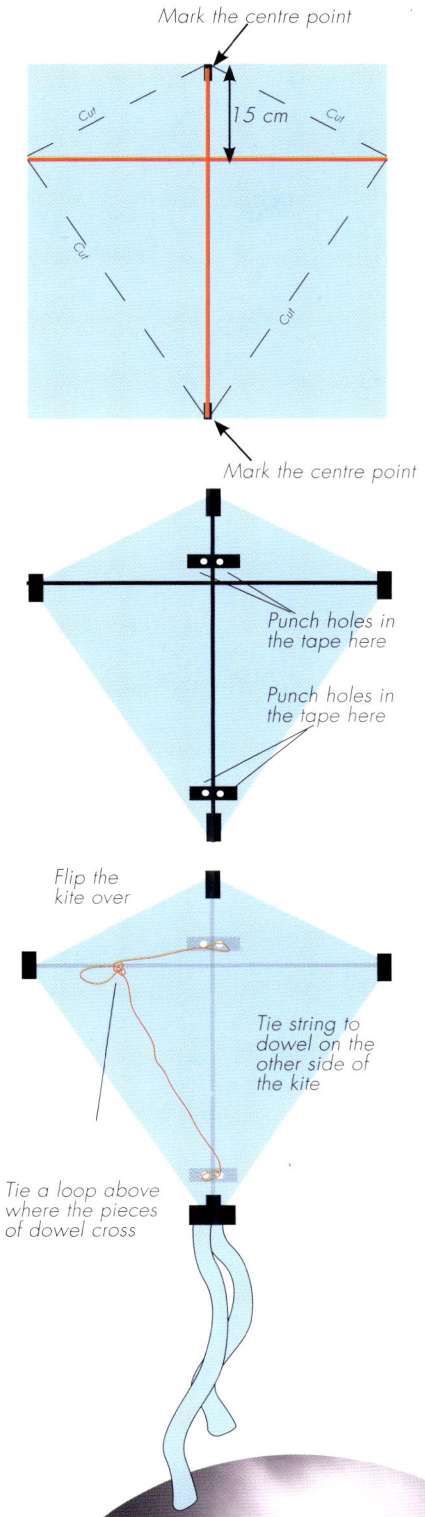

1 Use the texta to mark the centre of the top and bottom edges of the polythene square. Connect the centre marks with a straight line. Then measure 15 centimetres below the top edge and draw a straight line across the square. The lines you draw will form a cross (shown in red in the diagram).

2 Connect the points of the cross with straight lines (shown as dotted lines in the diagram) to make a kite shape. Cut along these lines.

3 Position the lengths of dowel exactly over the lines of the cross and tape the ends to the polythene using insulation tape. Also tape the centre dowel to the polythene 10 centimetres from the top and 8 centimetres from the bottom. Use a hole punch to make small holes in the last two pieces of tape on both sides of the dowel.

4 Turn the kite over. Cut an 80 centimetre length of string and thread one end through the holes in the tape near the top of the kite. Tie the string to the dowel. Thread the other end of the string through the holes at the bottom of the kite and tie it to the dowel as well. Then tie a loop in the string as shown.

5 Cut some thin strips of polythene about 50 centimetres long to make a number of tails for your kite. Tape on three for the time being. You may need to attach more to get the right balance when you start flying your kite (on the next page).

Electrifying

In 1752 Benjamin Franklin used a kite to study lightning and electricity. Sadly, several others attempting to do the same have been electrocuted. Do NOT fly a kite in a storm!

"Hawk" kite (continued)

Now that you have built the kite's basic structure, it's time to decorate it with the hawk shape and attach the ball of string.

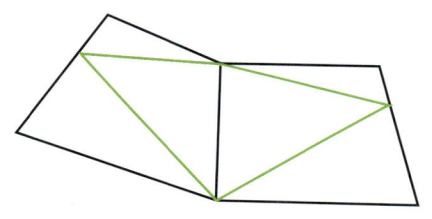

Fold

Cut through both layers

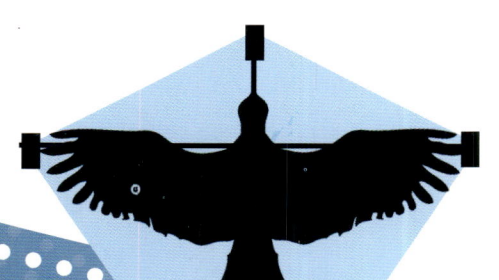

6 Cut a 52 centimetre length of coloured contact from the roll. Do not remove the backing paper but draw around the outline of the kite on the contact backing.

7 Fold the contact in half. Place the hawk template along the folded edge so that it fits inside the kite outline. Draw around the outline of the hawk template. Cut out the drawing with scissors and unfold it to see the full hawk silhouette.

8 Lay the kite flat on a table, with the dowel side facing upwards.

9 Peel the backing paper off the contact and apply the sticky side to the kite as shown. It should cover and stick to the dowel and polythene. The contact should help hold the dowel against the polythene and strengthen the frame.

10 Flip the kite over and tie the free end of the ball of string to the loop you made earlier.

Making good use of kites

Kites have been used for a number of purposes. In the 18th century, weathermen tied thermometers to kites so they could measure the air temperature high above the ground.

Wedge-tailed eagle

Now you can try to get your kite to fly! You may have to wait for a windy day and you will need another person to help you fly it.

Have the other person hold the kite while you hold the ball of string. Let out about 8 metres of string as you walk downwind. Gently pull the string until it is tight. Then ask the person holding the kite to throw it upwards into the wind. This may take a bit of practice, but once you get the hang of it, you will have a fantastic time watching your kite soar through the sky!

A tail's tale

If the kite zigzags uncontrollably, you may have to add more tails or take some off until it becomes more stable. Take care not to add too many tails otherwise the kite may be too heavy to fly.

40 MINS

Ladybird beetles

Make a bug catcher

Every day thousands of bugs scurry around in your backyard. It is a dangerous life for insects but they have developed some amazing ways to survive. To get a closer look at some of these tiny animals you have to catch them, but they are very good at not getting caught. Here is something you can build that will help you.

Things you will need ...

- A clear plastic container (the wide pill bottles available from chemists work best)
- A roll of gauze, insect netting or muslin
- A roll of insulation tape
- Plastic tubing (8–10 millimetres in diameter and 1 metre long)
- Some plasticine, modelling clay or playdough
- A pair of scissors

Ant

Small but easy to see

It is not wise to pick up bugs with your fingers, even if they are tiny. Trapping them inside a clear container helps you see them up close without injuring the bug or yourself.

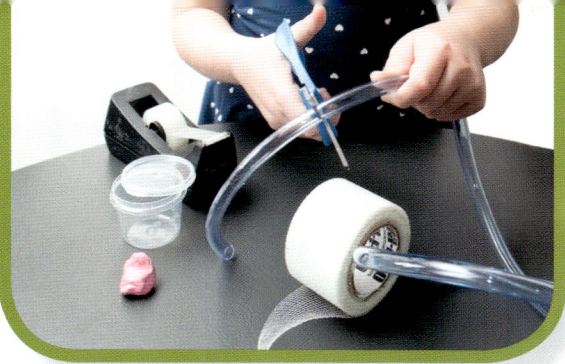

1 Cut the tubing into two pieces — one piece about 20 centimetres long and the other 80 centimetres long.

2 Tape a piece of insect netting over one end of the short length of tubing.

3 With adult help, cut two holes, each the same diameter as the tubing, in the lid of the container.

4 Push the netting-covered end through one of the holes in the lid so that the netting-covered end lies on the underside of the lid.

5 Push the long tube through the other hole. Use plasticine to make a seal around the tubing.

6 Put the lid (with the tubes inserted) on the jar. You should have one long tube for picking up insects and one short tube through which you can suck.

How to use it

Ladybird

The bug catcher is safe and easy to use. You don't even need to touch an insect to catch it. Suck gently on the short tube while you place the open end of the long tube close to an insect. The insect will be sucked into the container but not into your mouth. Always release the insect after looking at it.

1 HOUR

How to build an ant farm

Ant

Ants are fascinating insects to watch. They live in colonies made up of thousands of ants. Ant colonies are like little cities. Each ant has its role to play — some are builders, others find food and some keep the nest clean and tidy. When you set up an ant farm, you will be able to see how the ants go about building their ant city.

Things you will need...

- One large see-through container with a lid
- Another container or object that fits inside the large container leaving 15–20 millimetres of space between the two containers
- Garden soil • A funnel • A nail
- Garden trowel or shovel
- Some cloth or paper wrapping
- Ants (meat ants are good, but be careful if you choose ants that can bite or sting you)

Tunnels & nurseries

Ants often dig tunnels through the soil. By sandwiching soil between the two containers of your ant farm, you force the ants to make their tunnels close to the plastic where you can see them. You might even see their nursery chamber where the babies (ant larvae) are kept.

26

Ants tending their pupae and eggs

1 Place the smaller container inside the large container so that it leaves a 20 millimetre wide space (all around) between the two containers.

2 Use the shovel to collect some soil from your garden and tip some of it into the space between the two containers. You can use the funnel to help you get the soil into the small space. Fill the space halfway with soil.

3 Most Australian backyards have lots of ants. Sometimes ants hide their larvae under rocks or pieces of timber. If you find larvae, collect some of them along with a number of the ants and soil from the nest.

4 Put the collected ants, larvae and soil into the space between the containers. Use a nail to punch some holes (for air) in the lid. The holes need to be small to prevent ants escaping. Wrap some cloth paper around the container to keep it dark and let the ants settle. To view the ants, remove the wrap and look through the sides.

When you have finished observing the ants, return them to the same place you found them.

food & water

Like all living things, ants need food and water. Place a water-soaked cotton ball in the container so the ants may drink. Replace the cotton ball every day. For food, place a couple of drops of honey on a button and put it inside the container. Experiment with other types of food to see what the ants like best.

Ants

27

Weevil

Be a minibeast ranger

When rangers want to find out what animals live in their park, they have to take a wildlife survey. You can be a minibeast ranger and conduct your own scientific survey of the minibeasts (small animals) in your garden.

Things you will need...

Pitfall traps are great ways to survey (find out about) the small animals that live in your garden. The animals are caught in the trap without getting injured. You can see them, count them and release them unhurt.

- A healthy garden (vegetable gardens are best)
- Two clear plastic drinking cups
- Two small garden tiles or squares of plywood slightly wider than the mouth of the plastic cup
- Two small pieces of bacon rind, a slice of banana or some pineapple pieces — also try orange, potato, or a slice of bread
- Eight small stones or sticks

Millipede

Snail

Lots of legs

Millipedes are often encountered in the garden. When a millipede first hatches from its egg, it usually has only six legs. As it gets older, it grows more segments to its body. Since each segment has a pair of legs attached, it gets more legs the older it becomes.

1 Choose a spot in your garden that has moist, freshly dug soil, some young growing plants (young vegetables are best) and plenty of sunshine.

2 Pop two small pieces of bacon rind into the plastic cup. Dig a hole in the garden soil, big enough for the upright cup. Push the cup into the soil so that its rim is just below the soil surface, making sure no soil falls inside the cup. The cup will act as a pitfall trap when small animals walking over the soil are attracted to the bacon and fall inside.

3 Place four stones or sticks around the cup. Place a small garden tile or square of plywood on top of the stones so that it sits 20 millimetres above the surface of the soil. The tile will stop birds or other animals from eating the bacon or captured bugs.

4 Place some banana or pineapple pieces in the bottom of another cup. Then repeat steps 2 and 3. This trap will attract fruit eaters rather than meat eaters.

You can set up more traps using the other foods as well to see whether you catch different animals.

Keep a record

Beetle

Leave the traps in the garden for up to a week. Check them every morning to see what animals have crawled into them overnight. Look at the minibeasts without touching them. Identify which are fruit eaters and which are meat eaters by drawing them on a survey chart like this. Tip them back in the garden when you are done.

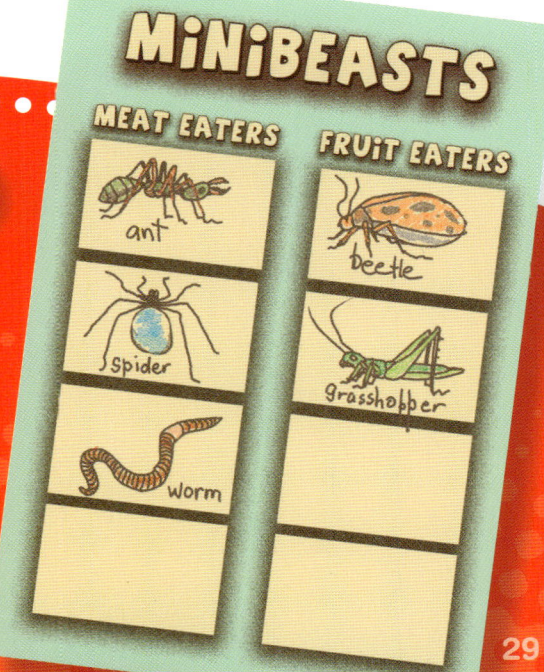

MINIBEASTS

MEAT EATERS	FRUIT EATERS
ant	beetle
spider	grasshopper
worm	

2 WEEKS

worm farm wrangler

Worms

Worms are great to have in your garden because they recycle plant material into soil. You can train worms to recycle your food and kitchen scraps, turning them into rich, fertile compost for your pot plants or vegetable patch.

Things you will need ...

- Three polystyrene boxes (from a green grocer)
- A lid or hessian sheet to cover the top box
- Lots of newspaper
- Compost and garden soil
- Lots of worms (red or tiger worms are best)
- Screwdriver
- Watering can
- Vegetable or kitchen scraps (no meat products, onion or orange or lemon peel)
- A brick

What worms want

Worms love to eat vegetables. The vegies should be chopped up very finely. Worms will also eat wet paper or cardboard as well as leaves and broken eggshells. Although they can eat meat, it's best not to add meat to worm farms in case it attracts flies and maggots.

1 Use the screwdriver to make eight small holes in the bottom of one of the boxes.

2 Tear several sheets of newspaper into shreds and use the shreds to line the bottom of the box with the holes. Add several (8–10) large handfuls of soil or compost. Lightly moisten the soil with some water from a watering can (don't make it too wet).

3 Add a handful of worms to the soil along with a small amount of vegetable or kitchen scraps. Cover the soil with hessian or newspaper to keep the surface moist and dark. Place a brick in the bottom of the other box and stack the holey, soil-filled box on top.

4 Let the worms settle for about a week before adding more food. Always keep the soil moist (but not wet) and don't overfeed the worms. Excess moisture and useful fertiliser will seep through the holes in the top box and collect in the bottom box.

Additional layers

Top box contains soil and worms

Bottom box collects liquid run-off fertiliser

Check the worm farm regularly. Add scraps and water as required. Eventually the worms will multiply and make more soil. When the first box is full, you can stack more boxes on top (add holes to the bottom of each new box). Place the food in each new box and the worms will climb through the holes to get to it. Always keep the top box covered with newspaper or hessian so it stays dark and moist. 31

GLOSSARY

ALTERNATIVELY Offering another choice.

APPROXIMATE To make a close guess or rough calculation.

CAST The solid material that fills the shape of a mould.

CHECKLIST A list with items that can be ticked or checked as they are collected.

COMPASS An instrument used to help people find the directions of north, south, east and west so they can navigate.

DISASTROUS A terrible event, as bad as if a disaster has occurred.

ENABLE To make possible or allow someone to do something.

ENCOUNTER To come across or see.

FASCINATING Very interesting.

FERTILISER A substance that contains good vitamins and minerals that help plants grow.

HESSIAN A type of thick, coarse material.

MAGNETISED Made to behave like a magnet.

MINIMISE Keep to a minimum; that is, to keep small or to lessen.

NATURE-BASED To do with nature and living things.

NAVIGATE To find your way around.

PARALLEL Side by side but never meeting.

PERMANENT Always there in the same place.

PLASTER OF PARIS A thick, paste-like mixture that is used to cover things, like walls, ceilings or craft objects, and that hardens when drying.

RECYCLE To wash and reuse empty bottles or any waste so that new products can be made from them.

REGULARLY Often.

HAWK TEMPLATE
FOR HAWK KITE ON PG 20.

Answers to footprint quiz on page 7:

1. Insect (beetle) 2. Bird (passerine)
3. Goanna 4. Bilby 5. Emu